The Bossy Boulder

how small is big and big is small

Written and Illustrated by
Monica Estill
Artist, Poet and Philosopher

Publication Consultants
Since 1978

PO Box 221974 Anchorage, Alaska 99522-1974
books@publicationconsultants.com—www.publicationconsultants.com

ISBN 978-1-59433-385-9

Library of Congress Catalog Card Number: 2013939670

Copyright 2013 Monica Estill

-First Edition-

Production Date: 5.13.13
Plant and Location: Printed by We SP, South Korea
Job Batch #041113

Dedicated to

Mary, Patty and Ethan

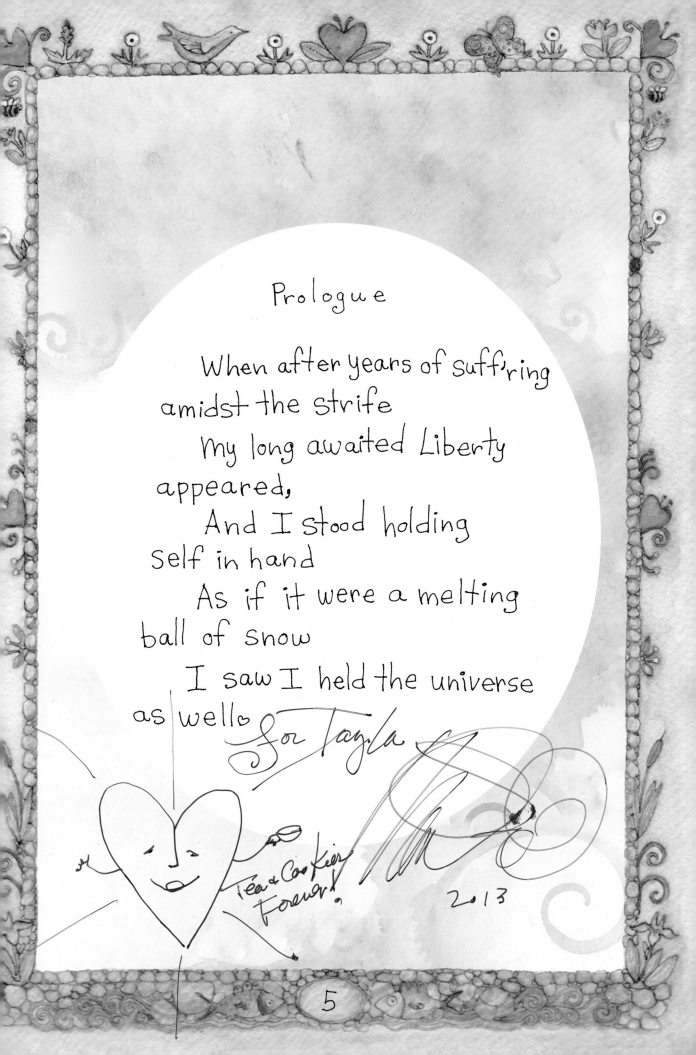

Prologue

When after years of suff'ring
amidst the strife
    My long awaited Liberty
appeared,
    And I stood holding
self in hand
    As if it were a melting
ball of snow
    I saw I held the universe
as well.

For Tayla

Tea & Cookies
Forever!

2013

There once was a large boulder who sat atop a high mountain.

He imagined himself to be the biggest boulder in the world and that he was on the highest mountain of all.

"This means that I am in Charge of the Whole World!", exclaimed the boulder.

That is why he became known as the bossy boulder for, thinking he was in charge-he thought it his duty to tell everybody and everything what to do.

He told the birds to stop flying and singing

and he told the trees to stop growing leaves.

He even told the sun to go down in the morning and to come up at night!

The boulder was so busy bossing
that he did not notice what was
really and truly going on around him.
He did not notice Time and Change
who were busily moving and doing
things everywhere.

Time and Change were the ones who were seeing to it that the birds flew and sang and that the trees grew leaves.

They were even making sure that
the sun came up in the morning
and went down at night.*

The bossy boulder did not even notice that bit by bit Time and Change had been digging and dusting the earth right out from under him until one day they pushed the bossy boulder right off his high place.

"Oh my", cried the boulder as he tumbled, "How can this be?"

Bang!

Bump!

Bump!

"He fell and as he fell he broke and got smaller. When he finally stopped he was very upset for he was no longer as large or as high as he had been before*

"This is aweful! This is Terrible!"
wailed the boulder, "Never has
such a bad thing ever happened
before!" He cried and cried.
He tried to pretend it was a
bad dream but it was not.

Little by little, as the boulder
calmed down he began to think,
"This isn't so bad, I will just pull
myself together and get right
back up on my mountaintop."
But try as he might, the boulder
was not able to move himself.

He called out to Time and Change,
for he certainly noticed them now,
"Why did you do this? The world
is counting on me to be in my
high place."

Time and Change said in reply,
"We must do the work which is
proper for us to do, which is to
help others do the things that
are proper to them."

This was not the answer the boulder had wanted.

"Hmm," he thought, "I guess I will have to go on with my work from right here."

So he began bossing the
flowers,
telling the grass
not to blow in the
wind and demanding
the butterflies take off
those great big wings.

While he sat there he noticed how Time and Change were helping the flowers to bloom, the grass to grow and the butterflies to have those big colorful wings and he was NOT happy about it.

"you are ruining my work!"

the boulder hollered in frustration.

Time and Change replied calmly,
"We must do our proper work and
help other things do what is
proper to them."

"Are you in charge
of the world?"

asked the boulder in a grouchy
voice~ but really wondering.

"No", they said,
"We do the work that is proper to us ..."

"I know, I know," grumbled the boulder, "and you help other things do what is proper to them."

With this Time and Change gave him a push.

Down he tumbled once again,

Bash!

Bang!

clatter!

Break!

Chip!

Smaller yet and much lower
down, the bossy boulder was
very confused

He could not get back to his high place on the mountain he was sure of that.

Time and Change would not help him. They did not see fit to push him up but only down and he could not push himself anywhere.

For a long time he just sat in his new spot and thought about things.

"He did not feel like bossing ~ he wasn't sure of himself anymore so he did not want to tell anyone else what to do.*

One day he realized something important.

"I am only a stone, a stone!

I am only a stone!"

as he thought about this
the boulder began to be filled
with joy*

"It is not proper for a stone to be in charge of the world.", he thought. "That would be absurd! Ha, ha," he laughed, "how could I have ever believed I was in charge of the world when I am only a stone? Ha, ha!"

Believe it or not, the stone, for now he was too small to be called a boulder, was happier and more peaceful than he had ever been.

"What is proper to a stone?" called the stone to Time and Change as they knocked him down further.

Clackity!

Smack!

Plunk!

He tumbled, he cracked, and he stopped.

"It is proper to a stone to tumble, break and stop we suppose," they answered.

Again and again he fell and broke.
As the stone became smaller and
smaller he trusted that this was
just the way things were supposed
to be. Finally after he had become
so small he was just a pebble
Clickity! Clickity!
Splish!
he ended up in the river at
the bottom of the mountain.

"Brr", it was cold and wet but the pebble did not complain for he trusted that this too must be proper to him.

After a while he found life in the river to be quite fun.

The rushing water lifted him up and set him down and swirled him round and round.

The pebble was so peaceful
and enjoying himself so much
that he paid no attention to Time
and Change who were working on him
even in the river.

As the pebble was swirled and
swooshed by the water, he was
"banged and bumped by Time and
Change so that all the while
he was chipping and breaking"
and becoming

Smaller
and
Smaller
and
Smaller

Finally, all that was left of him was a tiny grain of sand. He didn't realize he had become so small. He rarely thought of such things at all anymore. He just knew that he was sand among sand in the river, not bigger, not smaller.

By and by Time and Change
washed him up onto the shore
where he lay out on the beach
and dried out in the sun.

Then along came Time and Change in a great wind which blew over the shore and picked up the grain of sand. Swirly, Swoosh, Swirly, Swirl!

They carried him high up, up until he thought for one moment he would become a star in the sky.

Then down again, down, down
they came and set the tiny grain
of sand down very gently, way up
high on top of the mountain.

The grain of sand did not know he
was so high up. There was sand
there and that was all he needed to
make him happy, he knew he was
where he belonged.

One day as he was peacefully resting in his new place, he heard a tiny voice, "what's that mommy?"

a tiny cloud was pointing in his direction.

Chuckling the mother cloud said to her little one, "ask it what it is dear."

"What are you?" asked the baby cloud in his tiny voice.

The grain of sand nervously tried to think how he should answer but he found himself speaking in unison with all the other grains of sand...

...and so it was that while it seemed that the boulder was growing smaller and smaller he was really becoming greater than he had ever been before.